Pass the Ball, Grandad

DEBBIE WHITE

Illustrated by Terry McKenna

Oxford University Press

Oxford University Press, Great Clarendon Street, Oxford OX2 6DP

Oxford   New York
Athens   Auckland   Bangkok   Bogota   Bombay
Buenos Aires   Calcutta   Cape Town   Dar es Salaam
Delhi   Florence   Hong Kong   Istanbul   Karachi
Kuala Lumpur   Madras   Madrid   Melbourne
Mexico City   Nairobi   Paris   Singapore
Taipei   Tokyo   Toronto   Warsaw

and associated companies in
Berlin   Ibadan

Oxford is a trade mark of Oxford University Press

ISBN 0 19 918575 1   School edition
ISBN 0 19 918592 1   Bookshop edition

Printed in Great Britain by Ebenezer Baylis

Illustrations by Terry McKenna

Chapter 1

Every Friday after school, Tommy went to Grandad's house for tea.

Take-away fish and chips with extra-hot curry sauce. Brilliant.

Then, after they'd eaten, Grandad would get out his scrap album. He liked to talk about the old days.

'You wouldn't believe it now, Tom, but I was a champion footballer. Nearly got picked for England once.'

'Did you, Grandad?' Tommy would say. 'Tell me what happened.'

Well lad, it was like this...

Tommy never tired of listening, even though he'd heard it all before. It was great. Just the two of them.

But on Saturdays, things were different. Tommy got really embarrassed by his grandad then.

He hated the way Grandad would turn up at school football matches wearing his old team kit.

Shirt, socks, boots. Worst of all, those awful, long white shorts. Yuk. Tommy hated seeing Grandad's skinny, purple-veined legs sticking out. They looked horrible.

Chapter 2

'Can't you make him stop?' Tommy
asked his mum. She was
folding up his
goalie kit for that
afternoon's match.

'Tom, love,' said his mum, 'you
should be grateful he's not *your* dad.
When I was your age, Grandad used to
meet me and your Auntie Ruth out of
school.

'Then he'd make us dribble a
football all the way home. A mile and
a half of sheer torment. I still get
wobbly legs just thinking about it.'

'I wouldn't mind that,' said Tommy.
'It would be great. Can I dribble a
football all the way home on
Monday?'

But his mum wasn't listening. She
was miles away.

'Ooooh,' she shuddered. 'And there
was this little squirt called Trevor
Davies. He used to follow us, shouting
out rude rhymes.'

'What sort of rude rhymes?' asked
Tommy.

'I can't remember now. It was a long
time ago. Something about droopy
knickers, I think.'

What was rude about droopy
knickers? he wondered.

Then he said, 'Our new team coach
is called Trevor Davies.'

'Is he thin as a whippet?' asked
Mum.

'Yes!' said Tommy. 'How did you
know? And his nephew Mike Davies is
going to be our striker. It's not fair.'

'Is Mike a good player?' asked his
mum.

Tommy was torn for a split-second.

But he wanted to be truthful, so he sighed and said, 'Yes. He is. He's brilliant. Mr Davies says that one day soon, he's going to be spotted by a talent scout. Then one of the big clubs will whisk him away.'

An idea struck him. 'If Grandad was playing football now, do you think *he'd* be famous?'

'Maybe,' said Tommy's mum. 'But right now you've a match to play. So here's your stuff. Don't forget to put your muddy boots in the plastic bag. Oh, and it's raining, so I'll drop you off at school. Grandad will be at the match. He'll bring you home afterwards. All right?'

Blazing bananas, thought Tommy. No it wasn't. But Grandad loved to see him play.

By the time they got to school, the rain had turned to a fine drizzle.

'Do you think they'll cancel the game?' asked Tommy's mum.

'No chance,' said Tommy. 'Mr Davies said that even snow wouldn't stop it. It's a dead important match. Forest Hill Juniors hammered us last time. Eight-nil. It was terrible.

'We can't lose this one or we'll be out of the League Cup.'

'Oh, right. THAT important,' said his mum, ruffling his hair. She was about to give him a kiss, but he managed to duck just in time. Saved that embarrassment anyway.

But, oh no! There was Grandad jogging towards them. He had a football under one arm.

'All right our Tom?' he said. 'Get changed and we'll have a warm up.'

'Grandad,' growled Tommy, trying to look fierce. 'Everyone's looking.'

'Take no notice,' said Grandad. He was touching his toes, wiggling his shoulders, doing side bends.

'After all,' he went on. 'Not many lads have a grandad who nearly played for England. And don't forget that bit of advice I gave you.

'All good goalies watch the striker's eyes. Where a player's looking, is where he's kicking. OK?'

Tommy sighed. 'Yes, Grandad.' Then he sloped off to join the rest of the team.

As he got closer, he could see Mike laughing and pointing at him.

'Your grandad hoping to join the team?' sneered Mike.

Tommy scowled.

'You leave my grandad alone. He used to be a brilliant player.'

'Oh, yeah?' snorted Mike. 'Who'd he play for then? Tyrannosaurus Rovers... or was it Diplodocus Hotspurs?'

'I suppose you think that's funny?' hissed Tommy.

'We do lads, don't we?' said Mike. He turned to Tommy's team mates. Some of them sniggered.

'Now then. Stop that,' said Mr Davies stepping in quickly to calm things down. But he couldn't help smirking to himself... 'Tyrannosaurus Rovers? Ho, ho, ho. Brilliant.'

Tommy glared at Mike and Mr Davies. He felt all hot and angry. Then he remembered what his mum had said about Mr Davies. 'A little squirt with eyes like fried eggs.'

That made Tommy feel better.
Anyway, by then the ref had come
onto the pitch.

He called the team captains together.
They tossed a coin to see who'd kick
off. Forest Hill won. They decided to
kick into the wind.

Tommy took up his position in goal.
He joggled on the spot to keep warm.

He tried to catch the eye of Forest Hill's striker. He was too far away.

Instead he spotted his grandad standing on the side-lines.

He was talking to a short man wearing a smart raincoat. Tommy didn't know who he was, but he was smiling and shaking Grandad's hand.

Then Grandad pointed to Tommy and waved. He waved back.

Tommy was soon too busy with the game to wonder who the stranger was. Forest Hill were on form and playing to win. In the first fifteen minutes, Tommy had to make four saves!

Then it was save number five. Tommy remembered what Grandad had told him: watch the striker's eyes. See where they're looking.

Yes! Tommy dived to the right. His feet left the ground. His fingers reached out to catch the ball.

He had it safe, even though he'd cracked his elbow on the ground and was covered in mud.

Thanks, Grandad, he thought. Great advice!

Tommy felt good... but not for long.

He didn't see what happened, but 'Double-Decker' Dolan was suddenly rolling on the ground. He was clutching his leg.

'Double-Decker' was built like a bus. He was also one of their best players. AND Tommy's second-best mate.

Mr Davies ran onto the pitch. He seemed to be arguing with the ref.

His voice had gone all high and squeaky. He was jabbing his finger right under the ref's nose. But it did no good.

Double-Decker was carried off the pitch with a sprained ankle. Tommy's best mate, 'Worm' Wigley ran on to substitute.

The ref blew his whistle and the match began again.

Mike was playing really well. Tommy had to admit it. His ball control was so good, it made you want to cry.

He wasn't the only one to notice Mike. The man in the smart raincoat had too. Every time Mike had the ball, he'd write in his notebook.

But then Mike got too confident. He started showing off. He was running backwards shouting: 'To me. To me.'

Pass the ball to me!

He didn't see Worm Wigley right behind him.

They fell in a tangle of arms and elbows. The ref ran up to see what was going on.

'I think I've broken my arm,' wailed Mike.

'It's all right for you,' moaned Worm thickly. 'I think I've broken my nose. It's bleeding.'

'I'll give you "broken arm and broken nose",' screeched Mr Davies.

He ran over to where they lay in a heap.

'You need your heads banging together. You're a pair of great wet jellies. You've ruined everything. You see that man over there?'

Twenty-two heads turned to where
Mr Davies was pointing. But the man
in the smart raincoat had turned away.
He was shaking
his head.

'He's the scout for the local League
Club. I've been wanting him to look at
Mike for weeks. Now he's going away.'

Chapter 3

Mike started crying. Then he tried to stand up. 'I can play with a broken arm,' he snivelled. 'No problem.'

'Of course you can't. Suppose you were tackled. You'd end up breaking something else and then what would your mum and dad say?' Mr Davies was looking harassed.

Mike started crying again. 'Why do I have to play with such a load of idiots?'

'That's not fair!' said Tommy.

It wasn't anybody's fault.

'You're right there, son,' said Grandad. He'd come over to see if he could help.

'Just keep your nose out,' said Mr Davies.

'Well, Trevor,' said Grandad. 'I see you're just as rude as ever.'

Mr Davies sniffed and turned to Worm.

'And what about you, Worm... I mean William? Think you can still play?' he asked.

But by then, Worm's mum, Patsy, had run over. She was shouting at Mr Davies.

'Don't you speak to my William like that! Of course he can't play. I'm taking him down to the hospital. Come along, William… and don't drip blood in the car.'

'Now what?' said Mr Davies, looking over to the side of the pitch.

But there was only Paul Peakle, who never wanted to play. He looked as limp as a piece of wet lettuce.

'Jumping Jehosophat!' Mr Davies looked up at the sky. 'Just my luck.'

Then Tommy saw his grandad tap Mr Davies on the shoulder.

Oh no! thought Tommy. What's he going to say?

'All right, Trevor?' asked Grandad. 'What's the problem?'

'Nothing I can't handle,' said Mr Davies, trying to look as tall as possible.

'One lad short of a full team are you?' asked Grandad, with a lightning grip on the situation.

'Well...' Mr Davies began.

'Are you or not?'

'Yes I am,' said Mr Davies, looking as if someone had just popped his balloon.

'Let me play,' said Grandad.

'You must be joking,' said Mr Davies.

'Let me play,' said Grandad, 'and I'll have a word with the talent scout in the smart raincoat. He's still a big fan of mine.'

Mr Davies looked amazed. His mouth fell open.

'Right,' said Grandad. 'That's settled. But first we'd better get Mike seen to. Looks like he's in pain.'

'Thanks,' whispered Mike.

Tommy's lucky to have you as a grandad.

'You're right there!' said Grandad, smiling. 'Now where do you lads keep the spare kit?'

Chapter 4

Tommy could have died. There was Grandad squeezed into the Junior School strip.

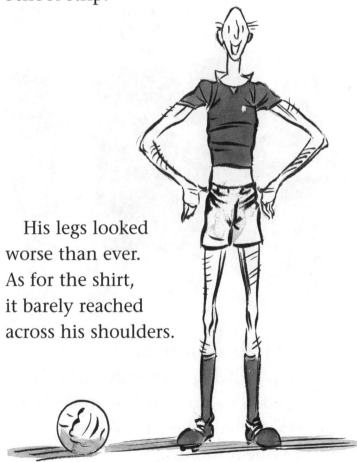

His legs looked worse than ever. As for the shirt, it barely reached across his shoulders.

'Now just hold on there,' said the ref, coming across to Grandad and Mr Davies. 'He can't play. He's a grown-up.'

If only, thought Tommy.

'I'm past being one of those,' said Grandad. 'I'm over the hill and going fast down the other side. I'll be seventy next month.'

'Oh, go on then...' said the ref. He blew his whistle.

'Let me at 'em,' said Grandad.

Tommy couldn't believe his eyes. His grandad was really good. In fact, he was brilliant.

Ducking and diving, dodging and weaving. His ball control was still masterly. At half-time, the score was one all.

Not bad. But Tommy could see Mr Davies was worried. He was chewing his scarf.

Then Tommy got the ball. He looked around. What should he do? He saw Grandad down the field.

He kicked the ball straight to Grandad's feet.

With only a minute to go,
Grandad saw his chance. But then
he came up against
Forest Hill's sweeper.
She towered over
him.

Terri 'Queen of the Foul' Taylor went
to tackle. But she didn't go for the ball.

Instead she caught Grandad behind the knee with her boot.

He was rolling on the floor, holding his knee. It was just outside the penalty area.

'She whipped me legs out from under me, ref,' cried Grandad.

'I never!' yelled Terri. But no one believed her.

The ref blew his whistle.

'He'll never be able to take that,' thought Tommy.

But Grandad leapt to his feet and placed the ball with care.

Seven of the Forest Hill team had made a wall in front of their goal. No one could get through that… or could they?

Their goalie was standing on the left. So Grandad kicked the ball with the outside of his foot.

It was a great shot. It swerved over Forest Hill's defenders. Bang! Straight into the top right-hand corner of the goal.

It was the last kick of the game: 2-1.

Grandad was a hero. The team even tried to carry him off the pitch, but he was too heavy.

They had to make do with slapping his back and shouting, 'Come on you Grandad.'

'Well done,' said Mr Davies, pumping Grandad's arm up and down till his head wobbled. 'I never knew you were so good.'

'I'm dead proud, Grandad,' said
Tommy. And he was.

'There's life in the old dog yet,' said
Grandad.

'Can we dribble your football all the
way home then?' said Tommy.

'Certainly,' said Grandad and he set
off.

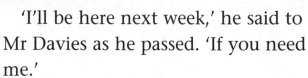

'I'll be here next week,' he said to
Mr Davies as he passed. 'If you need
me.'

About the author

I live in Leicester with two
sons, a husband, a sausage
dog, a cat, two guinea-pigs
and a goldfish. I love
chickens, but haven't got
any YET.

I wrote this story
because my youngest
son, Nick, is football mad. He plays in
goal, just like Tommy. My great-uncle Charlie
played professional football, had knobbly
knees and horrible shorts, like Grandad.

Now he's read the book, Nick wants to
dribble a football all the way home from
school too. No chance... it's five kilometres.

Other Treetops books at this level include:
Shelley Holmes, Ace Detective by Michaela Morgan
Here Comes Trouble by Tessa Krailing
Cool Clive and the Little Pest by Michaela Morgan
Snooty Prune by Pippa Goodhart
The Terrible Birthday Present by Angela Bull

Also available in packs
Stage 12 pack C   0 19 918577 8
Stage 12 class pack C   0 19 918578 6